THIS BOOK
BELONGS TO:

....

Unicorn Moonicorn

Nick Sharratt

Phoebe Tinkler

ALISON GREEN BOOKS

Unicorn.

Moonicorn.

Yellow-Red-and-Blue-nicorn.

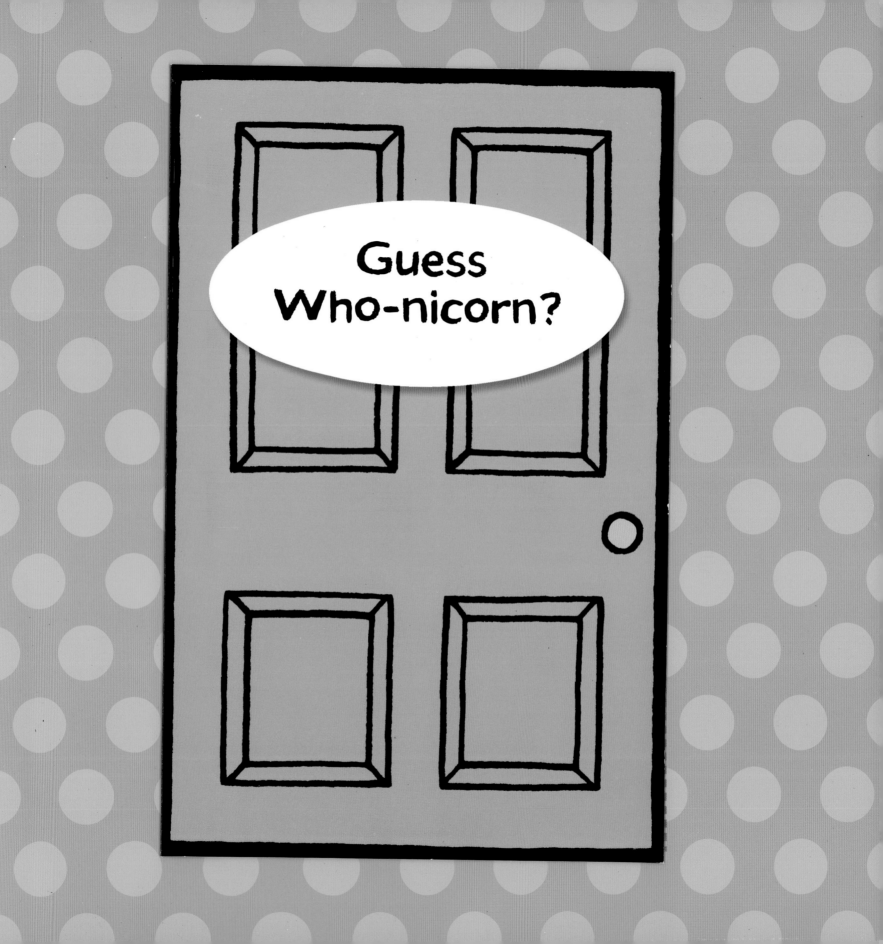

Knife-and-Fork-and-Spoonicorns.

Barbecue-nicorn.

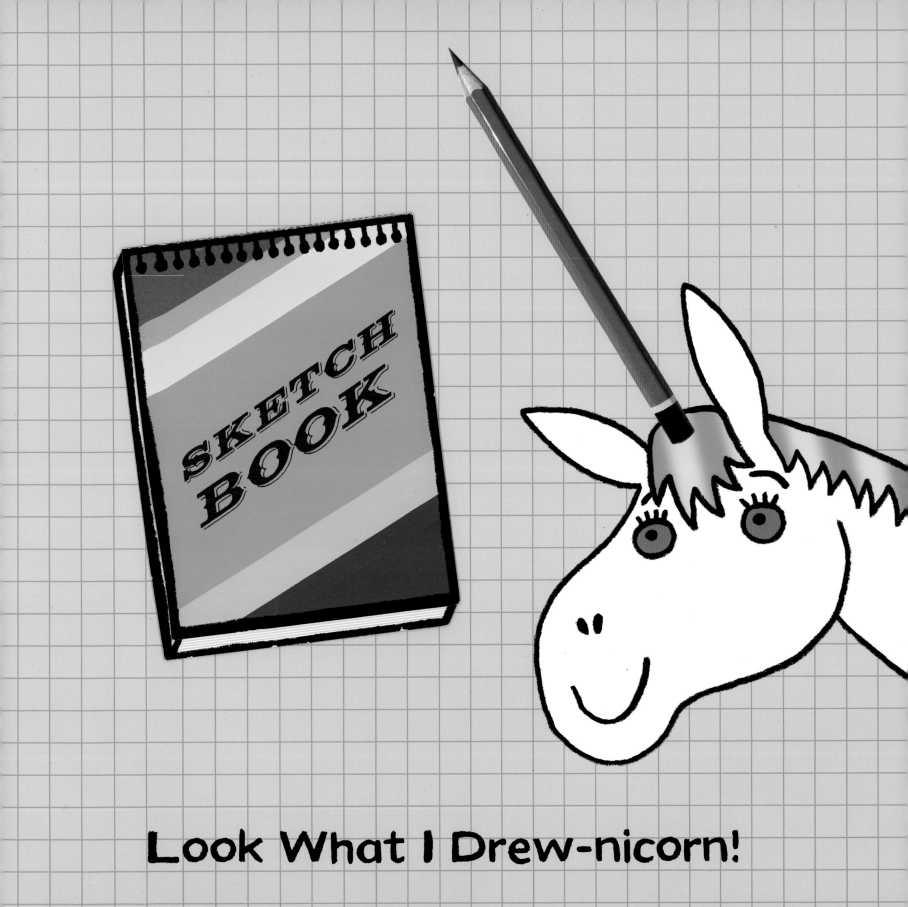

Look What I Drew-nicorn!

Old-icorn.
New-nicorn.

Covered in Green
Goo-nicorn.

Boo-hoo-nicorn!

Balloonicorn.

Fabulous
Hairdo-nicorn.

For Freya
P.T.

For Phoebe
N.S.

Published in the UK by Alison Green Books, 2022
An imprint of Scholastic
1 London Bridge, London SE1 9BA
Scholastic Ireland, 89E Lagan Road, Dublin Industrial Estate,
Glasnevin, Dublin D11 HP5F
www.scholastic.co.uk
Designed by Zoë Tucker

ISBN: 978 0 702303 52 4

13 5 7 9 10 8 6 4 2